NBJ - 1/93-3 - (2)
NBP 12/96 - 31 (2)
12/99 - 50 (12/99) (2)
12/01 - 56 (10/01)
4/10 71 (7/09)

JE '92

# JACKIE'S LUNCH BOX

by Anna Grossnickle Hines

Greenwillow Books
New York

Watercolor paints and colored pencils were used for the full-color art.
The text type is Della Robbia.

Printed in Hong Kong by South China Printing Company (1988) Ltd.
First Edition    10 9 8 7 6 5 4 3 2 1

Library of Congress Cataloging-in-Publication Data
Hines, Anna Grossnickle.
Jackie's lunch box / by Anna Grossnickle Hines.
p.    cm.
Summary: While big sister Carla is at school, Jackie
plays school, prepares a surprise for Carla,
and eagerly awaits her return.
ISBN 0-688-09693-X.    ISBN 0-688-09694-8 (lib. bdg.)
[1. Sisters—Fiction.]    I. Title.    PZ7.H572Jac    1991
[E]—dc20    90-39715    CIP    AC

For Rick,
who helped me know
who I am

My sister, Carla, goes to school now. She takes her
lunch box and waits on the corner for the school bus. I
have a lunch box, too, and I watch from the porch. She
always remembers to wave to me.
Then I have to play by myself. That's the hard part.

Today I walk in the backyard. All around the edge. I hit the pickets with a stick. Clickety-click, clickety-click. One, two, three, four, five, six, seven, eight, nine, ten, eleven. That's as many as I can count. Carla taught me how. She can count more.

One, two, three, four, five, six, seven, eight, nine, ten, eleven. One, two, three, four, five, six, seven, eight, nine, ten, eleven. I count all the way around the yard.

In the corner by the porch, I see a spider making a new web. I'm going to show it to my sister when she comes home.

One, two, three, four. I count up the
back steps and into the kitchen.
"Hello, Mama."
"Hello, Jackie."

I help Mama do the dishes. I put the clean pots in the cupboard with the other pots. The next cupboard has cans. Cans of soup, and cans of peas, and cans of beans, and cans of tomatoes, and cans of applesauce, and cans of ravioli, all crowded together.

The silverware goes in the top drawer. Knives and forks and spoons and big spoons. Lots of them. In the next drawer are dish towels, a whole big stack. Then pot lids, two big ones and two little ones.

In the last drawer, the one at the very bottom, there is just
one potato. All by itself. I put a can of tomato soup in
beside it, so it won't be so lonely.

At lunchtime, I eat my lunch out of my lunch box. I have
a peanut butter sandwich, a banana, two cookies, and
some milk. My sister's lunch is just the same, but she eats
hers at school.

"Do you think Carla misses us?" I ask.

"I'll bet she does," Mama says.

Mama reads a story just for me. She tucks me in for a
nap and gives me a kiss. "One special kiss for one special
girl," she says.
There is no one in Carla's bed except Midgie, her doll.
Midgie is lonely, so I put her in bed with me and Fudge.

When we get up, Mama gives me some raisins. She says Carla will be home in an hour. An hour is a long time, but not as long as a day.

I play school with Midgie and Fudge. I sit them in the chairs. I am the teacher. Carla says that's how it is in school. When she's home, she's the teacher and I have to sit in the chairs, too. I give Fudge and Midgie some paper and crayons, but I have to draw the pictures for them.

I tape the pictures on the front porch, so Carla will see them as soon as she gets home. She might even see them from the bus, if she's looking.

"How long now?" I ask Mama.

"Half an hour," she says. Half an hour is a long time, but not as long as an hour.

I look at the book that Carla knows how to read. She read it to me last night. She doesn't read fast, like Mama. Carla said, "It doesn't sound as exciting when I read it, does it, Jackie?" But I don't care. I like it when my sister reads to me. I want to make a surprise for her, and I know just what it will be.

I get my lunch box. I put in some crackers, some raisins, some lemonade, and four cups.

I take the old blanket into the front yard and spread it on the grass.
I take Midgie and Fudge and my lunch box and put them on the blanket. Then we wait.

The school bus finally brings my sister home.
Carla drew a picture for me, too.

And she thinks I made a wonderful surprise.